The Hamster of
the Baskervilles

Chet Gecko Mysteries

The Hamster of the Baskervilles

FROM THE TATTERED CASEBOOK OF

CHET GECKO
PRIVATE EYE

Bruce Hale

HARCOURT, INC.

San Diego • New York • London

visit us at www.abdopublishing.com

Reinforced library bound edition published in 2008 by Spotlight, a division of ABDO Publishing Group, 8000 West 78th Street, Edina, Minnesota 55439. This edition was published by agreement with Harcourt, Inc. www.harcourtbooks.com

Library of Congress Cataloging-in-Publication Data
Hale, Bruce.
  Chet Gecko mysteries / Bruce Hale.
    v. cm.
  Contents: [1] The big nap -- [2] The chameleon wore chartreuse -- [3] Farewell, my lunchbag -- [4] Give my regrets to Broadway -- [5] The hamster of the Baskervilles -- [6] Key Lardo -- [7] The malted falcon -- [8] Murder, my tweet -- [9] The mystery of Mr. Nice --[10] The possum always rings twice -- [11] This gum for hire -- [12] Trouble is my beeswax.
  ISBN 978-1-59961-461-8 (v. 1) -- ISBN 978-1-59961-462-5 (v. 2) -- ISBN 978-1-59961-463-2(v. 3) -- ISBN 978-1-59961-464-9 (v. 4) -- ISBN 978-1-59961-465-6 (v. 5) -- ISBN 978-1-59961-466-3 (v. 6) -- ISBN 978-1-59961-467-0 (v.7) -- ISBN 978-1-59961-468-7 (v. 8) -- ISBN 978-1-59961-469-4 (v.9) -- ISBN 978-1-59961-470-0 (v. 10) -- ISBN 978-1-59961-471-7 (v. 11 -- ISBN 978-1-59961-472-4 (v. 12)
  [1. Geckos--Fiction. 2. Lizards--Fiction. 3. Schools--Fiction. 4. Mystery and detective stories. 5. Humorous stories.] I. Title.
PZ7.H1295Ch 2008
[Fic]--dc22   2007028618

This one's for Ma Hale

A private message from the private eye . . .

Science. Ben Franklin couldn't juice it up, Madame Curie couldn't cure it, so let's tell the truth: Science is a snooze. In fact, the only science I like is the sweet science of detection.

Detection is my business. But you probably guessed that, if you know I'm Chet Gecko—the best lizard detective at Emerson Hicky Elementary. Unfortunately, my school doesn't give classes in private eyeing.

But it does have science—five days a week. Yuck.

What I know about science, you could just about fit into the Grand Canyon (and still have enough room left over for the entire population of China, a medium-sized brontosaurus, and a tuba).

Despite his best efforts, here's all I've learned from Mr. Ratnose's class:

—Some people can tell what time it is by looking at the sun, but I've never been able to make out the numbers.

—Rain is saved up in cloud banks.

—And germs come from Germany, while viruses come from Vireland.

But all my fourth-grade education couldn't prepare me for one case that started with science and headed off into the supernatural. Normally, I don't believe in that stuff. My idea of voodoo is Mom's mosquito-swirl ice-cream sundaes.

But when you're face-to-face with something from a late-night movie and you can't change the channel, you've got to ask yourself the important question: If it doesn't act *super* and it doesn't look *natural,* why do they call it *supernatural*?

1

A Heck of a Wreck

Some Mondays drag in like a wet dog, dripping puddles of gloom and trailing a funky stink. (Actually, at my school most Mondays are like that.)

But this Monday opened with a bang, like a fat frog fired from a circus cannon. And, like that frog, it turned into an ugly mess quicker than you can say *ribbet-ribbet-splat*.

No clue tipped me off as I trotted through the gates of Emerson Hicky Elementary mere minutes before the morning bell. One more tardy slip and I'd win a one-way trip to detention with the Beast of Room 3—not my idea of a dream vacation.

I dodged and darted down the halls past other stragglers, trying to beat the clock.

A sleepy second grader wandered into my path. Dazed as a meerkat on a merry-go-round, she stumbled along toward her classroom.

Za-yoomp!

I planted my hands on her shoulders and vaulted over the little shrew easy as slurping a gypsy-moth milk shake. My feet pounded onward.

Rounding the last corner, I was running full tilt—only seconds to go!

Old Man Ratnose's classroom loomed ahead. I bounced off the bright-orange door and skidded for my seat just as the bell went *rrriinnnng!*

And I would've made it, too, if not for Bitty Chu, the gopher.

Whomp!

Like a crazy cue ball, I hit her at top speed, ricocheted into Waldo the furball, and sprawled across Shirley Chameleon's desk. Private eye in the corner pocket.

Shirley blinked down at me with one eye, while the other scanned the room. Chameleons—what you gonna do? I saluted her.

"Hey, green eyes," I said suavely, "did you get the answer to that second homework problem?"

Shirley snorted and tossed her head.

"What's up, buttercup?" I said. "You've gone all yellow around the edges."

And she had. One thing about chameleons, there's never a dull-colored moment.

"Use your private eye, wise guy," she said.

Since when would Shirley skip a chance to flirt like the cootie machine she was? Something was rotten in the state of Ratnose.

I raised my head and checked out my fourth-grade classroom.

My jaw dropped. I didn't pick it up.

Mr. Ratnose's room was a mess. No—more than a mess, it was the Cadillac of cruddiness, the *Titanic* of trash, the Grand Canyon of chaos. If that mess were a monument, it'd be the Statue of Litterty.

Desks lay tumbled around the room like blocks in a cranky preschooler's playpen. Half-eaten papers covered the floor. Deep gashes raked the walls. A handful of seeds was scattered by the door. The seeds of destruction, maybe?

Most of my classmates stood gaping, saucer-eyed in amazement.

Bitty Chu tearfully fingered a wad of shredded paper. "Somebody's been munching on my math quiz."

Waldo the furball ran a finger along his toppled chair. "Somebody's been slobbering on my seat."

I noticed a jagged cut on the wall had mutilated my latest masterpiece, a safety poster. Somebody'd

been slashing up my artwork—and I guessed it wasn't Goldilocks.

What twisted hoodlum was responsible?

Mr. Ratnose stood knee-deep in the mess. His eyes were round as doughnuts, with a dollop of bitter chocolate in the middle. He sputtered like a deranged sprinkler head. Finally he choked out, "Who . . . is . . . responsible . . . for this?"

Nobody moved, nobody spoke.

"Who wrecked my classroom?" he asked.

Bo Newt nudged me. "Whoever it was, he had monster feet," he whispered. "I'd hate to have to shop for his tennies."

I looked at the muddy footprints. Bo was right. Whoever had made those tracks would wear shoes big enough for the football team to float downstream in.

"Who spoke?" said Mr. Ratnose. "Chet Gecko? Do you know something?"

With you as a teacher? ran through my mind. But for once, I passed up an easy joke. "No, Mr. Ratnose."

I tried to rise up on my elbows and tumbled off the desk. Retrieving my hat (and my body) from the floor, I got to my feet.

Mr. Ratnose's whiskers quivered like an over-strung banjo. He paced up the aisle to me, wringing his paws. "You're some kind of detective," he muttered. "Can't you find out who did this?"

I tilted my hat back and gazed up at him. "I'm some kind of detective, all right—the kind that likes to get paid. If I track down this goon, what's in it for me? Can I get out of doing my science project?"

"No," said Mr. Ratnose.

"Can I get free lunches for a month?"

"Not likely," said Mr. Ratnose.

"Can I—"

"How about two get-out-of-detention-free cards and a box of jelly doughnuts?"

"Done," I said. "Mr. Ratnose, I'm your gecko."

2

Intestines and Questions

We hit the cafeteria to watch a science film while Maureen DeBree and her janitors tidied up the mess in our room. My class flopped down at the scarred brown tables and stared blankly at the silver screen.

The movie was a classic: *The Splendor of Your Lower Intestines*. But I'd seen it before. After a few minutes, I sidled up to Mr. Ratnose, who was standing in the back, nibbling on an earwig eclair.

He bared his front teeth and put the pastry box behind his back. "Nothing for you until you catch that vandal," he said. My teacher, the mind reader.

"You insult me," I said.

"Not often enough," he replied.

I leaned back on my tail and crossed my arms. "Hey, we could sit here and swap insults all day. But if I'm gonna catch that hoodlum, I need a lead. Tell me..."

"Fire away," he said.

"Got any enemies at school?"

Mr. Ratnose's ears twitched. "Enemies—me? I'm a model teacher."

Yeah, I thought, *a model of Attila the Hun.* But I didn't say it.

Instead I asked, "Any former students who might hold a grudge?"

Mr. Ratnose stroked his whiskers. "Can't think of any," he said. "All my students love and respect me."

Boy, was he dreaming.

"Oh, wait," said Mr. Ratnose. He scratched a pink ear. "A few years back, I did flunk Erik Nidd. He wasn't too pleased, I recall."

"That's a long wait for a guy with a short memory. Anything else?"

He shook his head. "It must've been a bunch of hepped-up juvenile delinquents."

"I'll check it out," I said. "Do you—"

"Aren't you going to write all this down?" said Mr. Ratnose.

"No need." I tapped my head. "Photographic memory."

Mr. Ratnose raised an eyebrow. "Must've run out of film in math class," he drawled.

I coughed. This interview was going nowhere faster than a coyote in concrete booties. Time for one last question. "Who else has keys to your room, other than the janitors?"

"Oh, let's see," he said. "There's Principal Zero and the assistant principal. But that won't help."

I frowned. "Why not?"

"The door wasn't unlocked—it was ripped open."

"What?"

Mr. Ratnose nudged me. "That's enough for now. Watch the movie. You can detect at recess."

I wandered back and slid into an open spot beside Bo Newt. Up on the screen, a cartoony Captain Lunch had almost completed his heroic journey through the digestive system. I barely noticed.

"How about that?" I muttered. "Ripped open."

"*Shh!*" said Bo. "I wanna watch the story, find out what happens."

"Aw, don't worry," I said. "It all comes out in the end."

After the movie, we tromped back to our room. It wouldn't win any beauty contests, but Maureen DeBree and her crew had righted the wreckage. The classroom looked no worse than my bedroom at home—but that's not saying much.

Unfortunately, the janitors had also cleaned up the clues. I made a mental note to talk to Ms. De-Bree and strolled over to eyeball the gashed walls.

"Class, be seated," said Mr. Ratnose.

I kept walking.

"Chet Gecko?" said Mr. Ratnose. "Are you part of this class?"

Like I had a choice. "Guess so, teacher," I said.

Mr. Ratnose pointed at my chair. "Then sit down and join us."

For the next hour, instead of tackling the case, I had to grapple with grammar. Oh joy. English class can put anyone into a comma.

Then—*rrrring!*—at long last, recess. I straightened my hat and slid from my seat. Chet Gecko was on the prowl. First stop: the classroom wall.

Deep parallel slashes snaked down the woodlike lightning bolts.

I leaned close and sniffed deeply.

Aha! Splinters up the nose.

As I picked out the splinters, I noticed they smelled like peanut butter. Or maybe that was my fingers. (Eating peanut-butter-and-cockroach muffins will do that to a guy.)

Each groove was two fingers wide and deep enough to swallow an eraser. Whatever had made the gashes—tool, tooth, or claw—it was wielded by someone with a hefty grudge and some serious muscle. But why?

Maybe Mr. Ratnose's hunch about "juvenile delinquents" wasn't so far off base. Or maybe some sixth-grade mug had taken his revenge on my teacher for one too many detention slips.

Heading out onto the crowded playground, I kept an eye peeled for my partner, Natalie Attired. When you're taking a thug-country safari, you'd better have some backup.

Natalie was sitting on a bench with a joke book, cackling to herself. Aside from being a smart-aleck bird with a nose—er, beak—for trouble, she was a good dame in a tight spot: cool as a cucumber-and-ladybug sandwich.

"What's the word, mockingbird?" I said, walking up to her.

Natalie glanced up. "Chet, you gotta hear this one." In a voice like John Wayne's, she said, "A three-legged dog walked into a saloon in the Old West. He slid up to the bar, and do you know what he said, pardner?"

"I'm afraid you're going to tell me."

"He said, 'I'm lookin' for the man who shot my paw!'" Natalie leaned forward, wide-eyed. "Shot my paw! My *pa,* get it?"

I got it, but wished I hadn't.

"Hey, if you don't like that one, there's more..."
Natalie paged through the book.

"Never mind," I said quickly. "No time for wise-cracks when there's a case to crack."

My partner grinned. "Outstanding. Who's the client?"

"Mr. Ratnose."

She arched an eyebrow. "Hey, maybe he'll give you better grades if we solve the case."

"I couldn't pry better grades out of him with a pick and a crowbar."

"Well," said Natalie, "you *could* try doing your homework."

"And ruin my reputation?"

With a jaunty step, I led the way to the sixth graders' playground. It was a fresh case and a sunny day. It was good to be a detective, and I wanted to start the investigation right away—because crime waits for no gecko.

3

Meanwhile, Back at Tarantula

Erik Nidd was a bully's bully. His powerful tarantula body boasted eight thick limbs designed for shakedowns, punching, poking, and giving noogies. Just the sight of his fangs could make a first grader faint. And if that didn't work, Erik's B.O. could drop a horsefly at six paces.

Good thing he wasn't bright enough to power a night-light, or he would've *really* been dangerous.

Erik was easy to find at recess. We just followed the sound of whimpering. In a corner of the playground, the giant tarantula was dangling a blue-belly lizard by her tail.

"Please!" she cried. "I'll never do it again! Please let me go."

"Okeydokey," said Erik. He swung her around once, twice, three times—and let go.

The lizard soared like a superhero. *Thud!* She landed on her belly and scrambled away.

"Erik!" I called. "How's that lobotomy working out?"

He turned his many eyes on me. None of them held a friendly look.

"Whatchu want, peeper?" Erik sneered. "Flying lessons?"

"No," I said, "talk."

Erik crawled closer, if you can call it *crawling* when a tank-sized tarantula rumbles toward you. "Ya got nothin' to say that I wanna hear. Except maybe 'Here's my lunch money.' Haw, haw."

Natalie and I stepped back. When dealing with Erik, it's best to keep your distance—in the next county, if possible, but always out of reach.

"We want to talk about you and Mr. Ratnose," said Natalie.

"Ancient history," said Erik.

"My favorite subject," I lied. "I hear when you took his class, you and he weren't exactly best pals."

The giant tarantula made a gargling sound. I think it was a laugh. Two girls nearby decided to go play catch somewhere else.

"Ratnose and me, we don't exchange no Christmas cards," he said. "I had two years in his class, and it weren't no picnic."

Apparently, those two years hadn't taught him how much Mr. Ratnose hates double negatives.

I needled him some more. "How did you feel when he flunked you?"

Erik sidled closer. "I wanted to give him a big ol' smooch. Whaddaya think, ya moron? I hated his guts."

Erik's short fuse was burning down to the danger zone. Natalie and I exchanged a quick glance. We only had time for another question or two, at most.

Watching Erik closely, I said, "Someone trashed Mr. Ratnose's classroom over the weekend. Know anything about it?"

His many eyes went wide, and an evil grin split his face. "First I heard of it," he said. "But thanks, Gecko. Ya made my day."

One beefy tarantula arm reached out, whether to pat my shoulder or pick my pocket, I didn't know. But I wasn't waiting around to find out.

As I ducked, I noticed a dark blue tattoo on his shoulder—or where a shoulder would've been on a normal animal.

Natalie spotted it, too. "Nice tattoo," she said, backing up carefully. "Is it a sticker, or did your baby sister draw it?"

Erik snarled and scuttled straight at us. We scooted out of reach, then hightailed it for the safety of the classrooms.

He shouted after us, "Just watch yer step, ya... ya... big dum-dums!"

"Aw, you stole that line from Shakespeare," I shouted back.

When Natalie and I had put a portable classroom between us and the angry tarantula, I asked, "Well, what do you think?"

"I think I'm glad he's not a Mexican jumping spider," she said.

I put my hands on my hips. "His reaction, featherhead. Did you notice how he took the news about Mr. Ratnose's room?"

Natalie shrugged. "He won't be losing any sleep over it."

"But he didn't look guilty, he looked surprised."

"You're right," said Natalie. "So scratch one suspect. Now what?"

We stood in silence for a while. Two pigeons strutted past, heading for class.

I snapped my fingers. "Ah!"

"Thought of something?" asked Natalie.

"Yeah," I said. "I forgot to bring money for a snack. I hate when that happens."

"What about the case?"

"Oh, that. Simple: We visit the janitor and see

what trash she picked up from the classroom. Detective rule number two: When you hit a dead end, go back and check for clues."

Natalie cocked her head. "What's rule number one?"

"Always make sure you have a resourceful partner," I said.

She beamed. "I've got resources."

"Great," I said. "Can you loan me fifty cents for a snack?"

4

Humpty Dumpster

Before we could visit Maureen DeBree and go trash diving for clues, I had to dig my way through something even stinkier: history class.

A battered classroom hadn't stopped Mr. Ratnose. He stood at the blackboard, scribbling furiously and creating so much chalk dust he looked like a yellow tornado with a scabby tail.

As my teacher babbled on about the 100 Years' Bore (or maybe that was *war*—who knows?), I mulled over the case. A stray thought tickled my brain.

True, someone had trashed the classroom, but why did it have to be a cranky former student? Why not a cranky *current* student?

I surveyed my classmates. Frowns and bored looks hung on most faces, like a gallery of grumpitude. It could be any one of them, I thought. Even *me*.

Actually, I had a pretty good alibi. I knew where I'd been all weekend (except when I passed out after drinking five root beer slushies). And I could probably cross other names off the list—too wimpy (like Waldo), too sweet (like Shirley), or too prissy (like Bitty Chu, teacher's pet).

I was just sizing up the bad boys when a familiar name came to me.

"Chet Gecko?" said Mr. Ratnose. "Perhaps you could enlighten us."

My head snapped back to the front. I searched the blackboard to see what he was talking about. He'd erased it. I glanced right and left at my classmates. No help there, either.

"The answer is . . . um . . . ancient crustaceans?"

"Do you know what we're talking about?" said Mr. Ratnose.

"I haven't a clue."

His pink ears quivered. "Let's hope you're a better detective than you are a student," he said.

I'll spare you the rest. Let's just say I don't recall much until lunch, which that day was truly memorable—cricket casserole smothered in razzleberry-aphid sauce.

Just as I was mopping up my tray with a slice of mealworm bread, Natalie strolled by.

"Where you been?" I asked.

"I loaned my lunch money to *someone*"—I coughed and looked away—"so I had to go dig up some worms."

Worms. Yuck. I could never be a bird.

Natalie grinned. "Ready to get down to business, Mr. PI?"

"Ready as a rocket. Let's breeze."

We found Maureen DeBree roaming the playground armed with a light trash bag and a heavy frown. Emerson Hicky's head janitor, she was a lean mongoose with a serious thing for cleanliness. (Some said she had a serious thing for Mr. Clean, too, but that's another story.)

"Well, well, if it ain't the snoopers," said Ms. DeBree. "Hot on the entrail of some bad guy, eh?"

"Um, something like that," I said. "Ms. DeBree, we need your help."

"You and every playground in this school," she rasped. The janitor snagged a soda can and flipped it into the bag tied to her tail.

"We need to sort through the mess from Mr. Ratnose's room," said Natalie. "We're looking for clues."

"Oh, you wanna talk trash," she said. "Right this way."

As we walked, I prayed that she hadn't already emptied her bin into the smelly Dumpster. My hopes were punctured like a new balloon at a kindergartner's birthday bash.

"Dig in," said Maureen DeBree, pointing a fuzzy finger at the steaming heap. "Try that corner. It's fresher."

I held my nose. "Tell me, did you notice anything unusual when you cleaned the classroom?"

Maureen DeBree pulled a Q-tips swab from her utility belt and idly cleaned a furry ear. "Hmm," she said, "not so's I can dismember." She flicked the waxy swab into her trash bag.

"Oh, one thing," she said. "Whoever done it musta been hungry."

"Why's that?" I said.

"They munched a buncha sunflower seeds and left the shells behind. Slobs."

Natalie looked dreamy. I guess she thought seeds were even yummier than worms. But if you ask me, neither one is in the same league as chewy cockroach-nugget ice cream.

We thanked Ms. DeBree. She stalked off in search of evil litter, leaving Natalie and me to our Dumpster diving.

Ten minutes later, we were much stinkier, but still as clueless as when we'd started. We spotted my

classroom's rubbish, all right. But it would've taken Sherlock Holmes to find a clue in it.

Still, no reason the time had to be a total waste. I gobbled up a couple of flies circling the bin.

Natalie pointed at some trash and said, "What's that?"

I looked. "Moldy lasagna?" I asked.

"No, underneath—it's part of a sticker."

"*Hmm,* looks familiar." I leaned closer. The blue design reminded me of something...but what? The thought escaped me.

"Probably nothing," I said.

We kept digging halfheartedly. By then, the stink

of moldy hot dogs and sour milk was strong enough to build a house on. I was ready to call it quits.

But then I saw a piece of paper with a mysterious message.

"Hello, what's this?" I muttered. I passed it to Natalie. "Here's a puzzle for you."

She read the lines neatly printed on the page:

"Behold the tweety bird, so tweety
She flaps her wings so fleety fleety
And when she's walking down the stair
She shakes her Londonderry air."

"Some kind of secret code?" I said.

Natalie cocked her head. "Bad poetry. Whoever wrote this is flunking English."

My shoulders slumped. "Really?"

"Yes, really," said Natalie. "Now let's get out of this trash heap and into a good book. I need to study up for next period's quiz."

And so we quit the Dumpster patrol. But we took with us more than the gentle aromas of yesterday's rotting lunch. We wore the stink of frustration.

So far, this case had produced more dead ends than the film club's Gangster Movie Marathon. If I didn't dig up some suspects pronto, I could kiss those doughnuts good-bye.

5

Ferret Faucet

There ought to be a law against Science Fair. To me, it's a bigger waste of time than teaching a pig to yodel. Unfortunately, Mr. Ratnose didn't see it that way.

So there I sat working on a Science Fair project. I had wanted to build something useful, like a working model of a volcano or a deranged robot shark.

But did my teammates agree? Not those nimrods.

Instead, our project was a nerd's delight: "Nature's Little Batteries"—trying to make electricity from potatoes and other vegetables.

Personally, I thought the potatoes might have more juice than my teammates, if you know what I mean.

Igor Beaver bent to hitch some wires to a head of broccoli. He beamed at the rest of us. "We'll be the hit of the Science Fair. Hee hee!"

Hee hee, indeed. Guess who'd had the bright idea for "Nature's Little Batteries" in the first place?

My other teammates—Shirley Chameleon, Rynne Tintin, and a toad named Tiffany—gathered to check the connections. I pushed back my hat and sighed.

Then I figured, as long as we were there, I might as well do something helpful—like work on my case.

"Hey, how about that mess this morning?" I said casually. "Who do you think could've done something like that?"

Shirley cast me a sideways look. "Search me," she said with a flirty smile. She raised her arms for a pat-down.

"I'd rather not."

Rynne, a glum dormouse with Coke-bottle glasses, gave a snort. "It's so easy to guess," she said. "Check out whoever's had the most detentions from Mr. Ratnose."

I scratched my chin. "*Hmm*...and that would be...?"

"You!" said Rynne and Shirley together. They giggled.

"Cut the comedy," I said. "I'm on a serious case here. Who's got a grudge against the teacher?"

"What about Bosco?" said a small voice. It was Tiffany, so quiet I'd almost forgotten she was there. "Bosco is trouble."

She was right—how could I have missed it? Bosco Rebbizi was a surly ferret with a chip on his shoulder the size of a redwood tree. He'd started more fights than the bell at the boxing arena.

I tilted back in my chair and stretched, sneakily searching for that no-goodnik. There, two groups down. While the rest of his team prepped their "Magic of Velcro" demonstration of sticking power, Bosco was using Velcro to attach a KICK ME sign to a robin's back.

I'll say one thing: He didn't let schoolwork cramp his style.

Bosco was worth checking out. I decided to do just that at recess. Then a voice disturbed my thoughts.

"Uh, Chet," said Igor. "Your turn." He held out a mass of wires and a cucumber.

"Don't get cuke with me," I said.

I took the vegetable in hand. I couldn't wait till Science Fair was over.

When recess came, I shadowed Bosco out the door. He swaggered down the hall, bumping a classmate here, tripping a third grader there, lifting lunch money, and shredding shrubbery.

He reached the basketball courts without doing anything unusual. I leaned against a pole and watched the ferret swipe a basketball from a slow turtle. He stiff-armed her and began shooting, missing some easy hook shots that my blind grandmother could've hit in a force-five hurricane.

"Umm," said the turtle.

"Shaddap," said Bosco.

I sized up the situation. A private eye's first step in interviewing a suspect is gaining his confidence.

"Hey," I said.

"Drop dead," he replied.

So much for gaining the confidence, now for the advanced stuff.

"How about that stinker Ratnose? Can you believe how he's making us work for this lame Science Fair?"

"Beat it," said young Bosco. I could tell I was practically his best buddy now.

"Boy, I wish I could think of some way to pay him back. Like that trashed classroom—genius!"

I watched Bosco closely, but his ferret face revealed only bad temper and suspicion. His usual expression. He elbowed the turtle aside and dribbled closer.

"Thought you were working for Ratnose," said Bosco, "trying to catch the crook."

I shook my head. "Nah," I lied, "I'm stringing him on. I only wish I'd come up with that stunt."

Bosco's eyes narrowed into two black slits. "Why you telling me?"

"No reason. Just killing time."

"Yeah? Go kill it somewheres else."

He drilled the ball into my gut. It put a dent in my lunch, but I didn't flinch. Real private eyes don't.

"Catch you later," I wheezed.

Bosco gave me a thoughtful look. It didn't seem like he'd had much practice.

Then he spun and shoved the turtle. Bosco snickered when she tumbled onto her back and couldn't right herself. As the ferret brushed past me, his sour chuckles trailed him like stink from a smokestack.

I watched him go, then dropped the ball. My detective instincts told me Bosco was up to his furry ears in something. It smelled like trouble was brewing.

And there's nothing I like better than a fresh-brewed cup of trouble.

Still, when I turned to go back to class I couldn't shake the nagging feeling I'd missed some small detail, forgotten something.

"Hey," said the overturned turtle. "A little help?"

Oh yeah.

6

Hairy Plotter

Back in class, the heat was wilting students like a blast of buzzard's breath. I pasted a bland expression onto my face and let Mr. Ratnose's words roll off me like pill bugs off a pile of pasta.

Behind my eyes, that bowl of oatmeal I call my brain was busy trying to connect Bosco Rebbizi and the crime.

He had a motive. Anybody with as many detentions as me—we were neck and neck—had a bone to pick with Mr. Ratnose. But was that enough? And was Bosco strong enough to have torn open the door and done all that damage?

Hmm. As I pondered, I glanced over and caught Bosco watching me. His suspicions were up. But if I could just get closer to him, maybe he'd let something slip (something other than a strong right hook, I mean).

The bell rang. Anyone who doesn't believe in life after death should've seen that room full of corpses spring to life. My classmates stampeded for the door.

Bosco Rebbizi picked up his notebook and sauntered after them.

I waited a couple of beats, rose to follow, and nearly bumped into Mr. Ratnose.

"Well?" he said. "Have you caught that vandal?"

"Uh, not yet. But we've got several promising leads."

(That's detective speak for "not a clue.")

Mr. Ratnose bared his long front teeth and slammed a fist into his open paw. "I expect results, Mr. Gecko. And I expect them PDQ!"

"Hmm." I raised an eyebrow. "Pudgy, dumb, and queasy?"

"Pretty...darned...quick," snarled Mr. Ratnose.

I hopped like a quick bunny out the door. The corridor was ferret-free. Bosco had skedaddled. As I scanned the crowd, my partner sashayed down the hall in a gaggle of girls, cheerleaders to either side. Frenchy LaTrine, a sassy mouse, leaned past Natalie.

"Hiii, Chet!" said Frenchy with a giggle. "Need a study partner?"

"Put a pom-pom in it, Frenchy," I said. It never pays to let a dame get the upper hand.

I snagged Natalie and steered her aside. "Got time for a tail job?" I asked.

She looked behind her. "Am I missing some feathers?"

"Not that kind of tail job, birdbrain—following Bosco Rebbizi. I've got a hunch he's wrapped up in this caper somehow."

"Count me in."

"You fly the friendly skies; I'll beat the bushes."

"Who'll bop the re-bop?" she cackled.

I gave her my deadpan stare. "Just try to find him."

Natalie flapped out across the grass until she was airborne. Then she glided in ever-widening circles, trying to spot the ferret in the rabble of homeward-bound kids.

A spring breeze tickled my nose. Ah, spring, the season of Kleenex. I trotted across campus scanning the crowds. No Bosco.

Near the sixth-grade classrooms, I turned a corner and bonked into a teacher. *"Oof!"*

A box of plastic beakers and science supplies went tumbling. I skated over them as gracefully as a hippo in a tutu—swaying right, left, right—then tumbling onto my tail.

A fuzzy black foreclaw reached down. It was connected to a stubby arm, and that led up to a face with thick glasses and a nose like an exploding muffin. It was Ms. Burrower, a sixth-grade teacher. She was a mole.

"Are you hurt, laddie?" she said.

I shook my head cautiously. Nothing rattled that hadn't rattled before.

"All right, then. Up you go." Ms. Burrower pulled me to my feet.

Keeping an eye peeled for Bosco, I quickly helped her gather the supplies. "Working on a cure for boredom?" I said.

"Nah, just a wee experiment for the fair." Ms. Burrower was the mastermind behind the school's Science Fair—in fact, she was supposed to win some Top Teacher award for it. Consequently, Ms. Burrower wasn't at the top of my best buddies list.

As I dropped the last beakers into her box, the big mole squinted down at me. "And how is your science project going?"

I looked away. "Gee, is that my mom calling? Gotta go!" I split without a backward glance.

Across the playground, Natalie was gliding over the portable buildings. I headed over. She met me halfway.

"Any luck?" I called.

"Jackpot!" she said, circling above me. "It's a regular punk-a-palooza behind the portables. Meet you up top!"

One of the benefits of being a lizard detective is superior wall-crawling ability. In two shakes and a slither, I was crouching atop one of the portables with Natalie.

We crawled silently and peeked over the far edge. Below us lurked enough roughnecks to cast a road show of "Oliver Twisted." Besides Ol' Ferret Face, Bosco Rebbizi, a dirty dozen members of the detention hall of fame lounged in the shade. They were doing regular tough-guy things: carving their initials in the wall, polishing their brass knuckles, sharpening their teeth, and playing the odd game of bridge.

"What fresh foolishness is this?" I muttered.

"I love it when you get literary on me," whispered Natalie.

As we watched, Erik Nidd rumbled around the corner and joined the group like a sultan greeting his subjects. After the usual boot licking (claw licking?), they formed a chattering circle. Erik cleared his throat.

"Pipe down, ya mugs," he said. They piped. "Today we welcome a new member, and I gotta say I'm proud of him."

At this, Bosco sauntered up to Erik. The giant tarantula pumped the ferret's hand, pounded him on the shoulder, and dug something out of a nearby backpack—and he didn't use even *half* of his arms.

"Bosco Rebbizi is a punk's punk," said Erik.

The motley crew responded with cheers and hoots. Erik continued.

"He aced his test—ya shoulda seen the stunt he pulled! Anyhow, Bosco is now a what-ya-call, full-fridged member of the Dirty Rotten Stinkers." Erik produced a stick-on tattoo and slammed it onto Bosco's shoulder with more force than absolutely necessary.

Bosco staggered but didn't flinch. It wouldn't have been the punkish thing to do. The surly ferret flexed and showed off his tattoo while the gang applauded.

I didn't notice much of a muscle. But I did notice the tattoo.

So did Natalie. "That's the same one Erik was wearing," she muttered.

"And the same one we found mangled in the trash bin," I whispered.

The pieces were starting to fall together like spider eggs into an omelette. All we needed was more evidence linking Bosco to the vandalism, and the case was closed.

I could almost taste Mr. Ratnose's jelly doughnuts. But then (as they say in California), my karma got a flat tire.

A stray breeze sent some dust up my nose, and— "Ah...ah...*choo!*" I sprayed a sneeze like a lisping platypus spelling Mississippi.

Natalie and I ducked out of sight—too late.

"Hey!" said Erik. "Who's up there? Kurt Replie, check it out."

"Cheese it!" I hissed. Natalie took to the air as I hightailed it back across the roof and down the opposite wall. When I hit the ground, I jumped away from the building, then plunged my hands into my pockets and shuffled along.

"You!" a voice shouted.

I turned innocently. "Who, me?"

A cranky rat stood on the roof. "Yeah, you," he said. "What are you up to?"

"Oh, about six inches," I said. "I'd like to be taller, but platform shoes are so uncool."

The rat snarled and turned away. I grinned.

With any luck, I thought, we should find the evidence and polish off this case by lunchtime tomorrow. Poor sap. Little did I know that the fickle foot of fate would kick the card table of detection, sending the puzzle pieces flying.

(Ooh, not bad. I'll have to use that in my English homework sometime.)

7

Hook, Line, and Stinker

My good mood lingered until the next morning, like the aftertaste of a garlic-and-stinkbug pizza. I was fat, green, and sassy, and I didn't care who knew it.

I had a plan.

Natalie met me by the flagpole before school, and we headed back toward the portable buildings. "You think they'll let us join?" she asked.

"Of course," I said. "With our acting skills, they won't suspect a thing."

Natalie ruffled her feathers. "But what if it's a dead end? Do you really think Bosco is our culprit?"

"Do flies fly? Do ducks duck? Do skunks believe in Stenchy Claus?" I said. "Of course he's our culprit. We just have to get close enough to prove it."

We neared the portables. A familiar grumpy rat with advanced tooth decay leaned against the wall. A lookout.

I turned to Natalie. "Ready for some playacting?"

She grinned. "You kidding? As one cowboy said to the other, all the world's a stagecoach."

Sometimes, I just don't get mockingbird humor.

"Back off, bozos!" snarled the rat. "This is Stinkers territory."

"We know, we can smell it," I said. "Are you Kurt Replie?"

The rat bared his yellowed teeth. "Who wants to know?"

"We wanna join the Stinkers," said Natalie in her best tough-gal voice.

"Oh, you do?" said Kurt. "Well, la-di-da."

"And boola-boola," I said. "Where can a guy fill out an application form?"

The rat snickered. "Wise guy, huh? Step over here. We know how to handle wise guys."

Kurt led us behind the building. Just like yesterday, the Dirty Rotten Stinkers lounged in the shade, doing what they did best: stinking.

"These mugs say they wanna join the gang," said the rat.

The gang laughed. At least I think it was laughter. It sounded more like a pack of hyenas choking on their Cheerios 'n' Carrion breakfast.

I did my best to look like a punk. "Yo, Bosco," I grunted.

The ferret squinted at me. "You again?" he said.

The giant tarantula, Erik Nidd, eyed Bosco. "Ya know this twerp? He's a peeper."

"I know," said the ferret. "He's in my class. But who's the bird?"

Natalie hawked and spat. "The name's Nat the Knife," she sneered. "Meanest blade this side of the Pecos."

Bosco squinched up his face in puzzlement. On him it looked natural.

"Uh, she's with me," I said.

"Oh." The ferret circled us. "So you wanna join the Dirty Rotten Stinkers."

"But are you tough enough?" said a bloated bullfrog. She drained her soda can, belched, and crushed it on her forehead with her tongue.

"Not bad," I said. "Do you recycle, too?"

Kurt stuck his pointed snout in my face, treating me to a close-up of his yellow incisors. Lovely. I guessed that he and Mr. Tooth Decay were on a first-name basis.

"You can talk the talk," he said, "but can you walk the walk?"

Natalie leaned in. "You guys have a special gang walk?" she asked. "It's not the Shuffle-Off-to-Buffalo, is it?"

Erik grunted. "Anybody can lip off," he said. "Are ya bad enough to pass our test?"

"You kidding?" I said. "We put the *r* in rat fink, the *b* in bad, and the *d* in delinquent."

"And if you put 'em all together, they spell *rbd*!" Natalie grinned.

I shot her a warning look. "If we pass the test, can we do some cool stuff, like trashing Mr. Ratnose's room?"

Bosco chuckled. His expression was as hard to read as Chinese pig Latin. "We'll see," he said. "If you pass."

"Aw, you're not gonna let 'em try out, are you?" said the rat. "They're a coupla goody-two-shoes detectives."

Erik stretched four of his legs and yawned widely, flashing fangs. "One way to find out," he said. "And if they're spyin', they're dyin'."

My tail curled into a knot. I didn't like the sound of that. But we'd gone too far to turn back.

"Bring on the tests," I said.

Our first assignment: Swipe something valuable from our teacher's desk and bring it to the gang at recess. It sounded easy enough.

If I had to bend my morals to catch a crook, then so be it. A private eye does what's needed. (And hopes he can return the valuables later.)

As the morning passed, I studied Mr. Ratnose's desk. It was littered with papers and books and stuff—nothing valuable there. (Although I did consider stealing back my bogus book report on *Hairy Plotter and the Emperor's Bone*.)

A small item was best. His cheese wedge? Naw. His car keys? No, I'd get in real trouble. It had to be something—

"Chet Gecko," said Mr. Ratnose. "The answer is . . . ?"

"Uh, blowin' in the wind, teacher."

He shook his head. "If you don't bother to read the homework, can't you at least pay attention in class?"

I didn't know the answer to that one, either. Bitty Chu piped up with, "It's an adjective, Mr. Ratnose," and the class moved on.

The clock ticked off the minutes to recess.

I wanted to slip Mr. Ratnose a note telling him about my theft. But every time I looked around, Bosco Rebbizi was watching me like a cat after a tuna sandwich.

Recess came. Time to make my move.

Kids began shuffling outside. I hustled up to the front of the room.

"Oh, Mr. Ratnose," I said, pretending to search for something. "Where is the—"

I turned around, sweeping papers and books off his desk with my tail.

Whump! They cascaded onto the floor.

"Oops!"

"Look what you've done," said Mr. Ratnose. He bent to pick up the mess. Bosco watched us from across the room.

In a hurry, I snatched the first thing I could—Mr. Ratnose's pointer stick. But where to hide it?

I stuffed the stick down the back of my coat. "Heh, clumsy me," I said. "I, uh, better go out and investigate now."

Mr. Ratnose straightened with an armload of papers. His eyes narrowed. "Chet Gecko?"

I backed toward the door, bowing slightly. My hat lifted—the stick! I jammed the hat back down.

"So, I'll, uh, see you later."

Mr. Ratnose sighed. "I'm afraid so," he said.

Backing outside, I turned to find myself belly to belly with Bosco.

"So far, so good," he said. "See ya at the portables."

I watched him swagger away, my heart beating like a rock-and-roll drummer on an M&M's rush. Sweat glistened on my forehead. Stepping off after Bosco, I reflected.

Good thing I was a private eye. I could never lead a life of crime—with the stealing, cheating, and lying. It's harder on the nerves than three days of standardized testing.

8

The Frog Who Cried Wolf

The scene behind the portable buildings was livelier than a barrel full of wolverines going over a waterfall. The gang hooted at my prize.

"A *pointer*, woo!" sneered Kurt Replie the rat. "Check out the big bad gecko."

Natalie had stolen an apple from her teacher's desk. Probably put it there herself in the first place.

But we passed the test. Then we got a shock: It was only the first. Our next assignment was to make some *really* bad mischief. Joining this gang was harder than stale centipede biscuits.

"Ya don't get to hang out with the Stinkers till you pass all the tests," snarled the rat. He was really starting to bug me. "Am-scray, uster-bay!"

"Okely-dokely-ay, oron-may," I said. "Come on, Natalie."

We made tracks while Kurt was still trying to decode my insult. Never try to out–pig Latin a master etective-day.

As Natalie and I walked down the hall, she peeled off toward the vending machines. "See you at lunch," she said.

"Going to replace a certain apple for a certain teacher?"

The way she grunted and kept walking told me I'd hit the mark.

I strolled to my private thinking parlor, under the shade of the scrofulous tree. Carefree kids played jump rope nearby, but I didn't see.

Outfoxing a ferret was the problem that tied up my mind.

I was so deep in thought, I didn't even notice what was behind me until too late.

Fa-tchoom! Something small and fast hit me, sprawling me onto the sand.

"Oh Chet, oh Chet, oh Chet!" said Popper the tree frog. She bounced up and down on my back like a pint-sized pogo stick. "There you are! I've got a hot, a hot case for you! Wanna hear it?"

"If you'll—*oof!*—get off my—*umf!*—back."

She turned a double somersault and landed a few

feet away, vibrating like a hyperactive bowl of lemon-lime Jell-O.

I spat sand. "Now, what's the—*ptah!*—story?"

Popper's eyes swelled like a pair of overpumped volleyballs. "Someone saw a great, big ham sand wolf—a big, great hamster wolf—"

"A what?" I said.

"A were—"

"A who?"

"A monster!" she said.

It sounded like Popper was a few fries short of a Happy Meal.

"You saw a monster? Been mixing firefly pizza and late-night TV, eh?"

Popper shook her head so fast, she almost lost her nose. I had to look away to keep from getting dizzy.

"No, no, no," she said. "Not me—my friend's friend's friend. She came to school early-early, before the moon set. Then, all of a sudden, this big big monster—big and hairy—came running and howling."

I squinted at her. She was serious. "Sure it wasn't Principal Zero chasing an ice-cream truck?" I asked.

"She says it was a monster, I swear, I swear. A cross between a werewolf and a hamster, with feet like a giant." She bounced up and down like a Super-ball in a paint mixer.

"Look, short stuff. What do you want me to do—sign you up for the Famous Monsters fan club? I've got bigger bugs to fry."

I turned away from Popper's pout and hoofed it back to class. But then something she said tickled my detective senses. *Feet like a giant,* eh? I'd seen giant pawprints yesterday, in my wrecked classroom.

It was probably nothing, but a wise private eye follows all leads.

I hotfooted it toward Ms. DeBree's office. With any luck, I could ask her about the were-thingy, then check in on Bosco before the bell rang.

R-r-r-ring!

With any luck.

But this private eye's luck was as short as a vice principal's temper. Back to class I went.

9

For Badger or Worse

One and a half mind-numbing hours later, yet another bell turned us loose for lunch. Natalie met me in the cafeteria line.

"Hey, there's our prime suspect," she said, indicating Bosco Rebbizi and his friends at a nearby table. "Wanna eavesdrop?"

"All in good time," I said. "They're serving french-fried potato bugs today."

After loading up our trays, we headed for a table by Bosco and his bad boys. It wasn't hard to find a seat. Kids shunned the area like you could catch ten pages of math problems just by breathing the air.

Natalie and I kept our heads down and ate. Kurt Replie tried giving me the evil eye, but it was defeated by his hungry stomach. He went back to eating.

Soon my lunch had disappeared like a snowman in a hot tub. I raised my detective radar. Nothing much on the screen.

Bosco caught my eye. "Hey, Gecko. Figure out your stunt yet?"

"Not yet," I said. "By the way, what was yours?"

Bosco wagged a finger. "Unh-uh-uh," he said. "No cheating. It's gotta be your own idea."

How ironic. To become a Dirty Rotten Stinker, you had to play fair.

I decided not to share this with Bosco. No sense in confusing him.

The ferret and his low-rent pals scarfed their last potato bugs, carved their last graffiti, and got up to leave.

I leaned toward Natalie. "Stick close to them," I muttered.

"Why?" she asked. "Where are you going?"

"I'm off to see a mongoose about a werewolf."

Natalie shook her head. "Sometimes I don't get you."

"Sometimes I don't get me, either," I said. "But I'm all I've got."

So far, this case had thrown me for a loop. After all this time investigating Bosco, my only progress was in becoming a Stinker. But I knew someone who could help me catch up: Maureen DeBree, neat freak and all-around know-it-all.

I trotted down the hall toward her office.

Bap, bap, bap! I rapped on the graffiti-proof door. "Ms. DeBree?"

The door swung open. A gray-furred badger in rumpled overalls filled the doorway. My head tilted back.

Calling him large would've been like calling World War II a slight disagreement—it missed the mark by a bit. This guy was big enough to have his own personal zip code.

"I ain't Ms. DeBree," he rumbled.

"I noticed. When will she be back?"

The badger wiped his nose with a greasy rag. "What do I look like, her secretary?"

Actually, he looked like an unmade bed with a bad attitude. But he didn't need to hear that. I asked, "Maybe you can help me? It's about that trashed classroom . . ."

The badger's beady eyes narrowed. His scowl could have curdled a passing kindergartner's chocolate milk. "You're a nosy one," he said. "Know what happens to nosy kids?"

"They grow up to be Pinocchio?" I said.

He waved a thick paw before my face. His claws looked like a matched set of samurai swords.

"Nosy kids lose their noses," said the badger. "Get the picture?"

I backed up. "In widescreen, with surround sound."

No point in pumping a mug like that for more information. He'd only end up trying to break you in two and spread you on toast.

I nodded. "Nice meeting you, Mr. . . . ?"

"The name's Luke Busy," he growled. "Now beat it."

I sneered. He sneered back. His sneer was meaner. I beat it.

10

Wholly Mole-ly

Why was a bad-tempered brute like Luke Busy working for Maureen DeBree? That question bounced around my noggin while I searched for the head janitor.

He'd stonewalled me like a professional bricklayer. Was the badger trying to cover up something? Or was it just the effect of my charming personality?

No matter. I had bigger questions to ask Ms. DeBree. And there she was, striding down the hall on trash patrol.

Gzitch! Gzatch! Her spike lashed out and nailed two gum wrappers. I'd hate to be a piece of litter in her path.

"Ms. DeBree!" I called. "Got a minute?"

"Hah?" She looked around, bright eyes flashing. "Oh, it's the great defective."

"That's *detective*," I said, walking up to her. "Listen, have you seen any sign of a werewolf on campus?"

She frowned. "No, and I better not, neither. Those things make a rotten mess when they shed. Why you ask?"

"Oh, never mind. Just a wild—"

Ms. DeBree waved her spike. "Hey, I get something for you."

"For me? Aw, you shouldn't have."

"Not a present, you knucklehead. Information."

"I'm all ears." (Actually, this was stretching it; geckos don't have ears.)

Marching along, the janitor speared a soda can, a wrapper, and a paper cup—triple play. "You was asking about the discomboobulated classroom," she said.

I walked beside her. "Yeah?"

"Well, I seen another one."

"What?"

Ms. DeBree slid the trash off her spike into a plastic bag. "Yup. This morning, Ms. Burrower's sixth-grade classroom looked like the morning after Super Bowl Sunday." She shook her head and tramped on. "Hoo, what a mess."

"But..."

I stumbled after her. My head spun as ideas collided. If Bosco had trashed Mr. Ratnose's classroom, why had he wrecked Ms. Burrower's room, too? If he hadn't, then who had—another Dirty Rotten Stinker?

Maureen DeBree shot me a glance from under her bristly eyebrows. "You okay? Looks like you need some mouth-to-mouth regurgitation." The image made me want to throw up my hands and say, "Pee-yew!"

"I stink so," said another voice, reading my mind. Natalie had just strolled up behind me. You could smell her puns a mile away.

"But who . . . ?" I said.

The janitor led us out across the grassy playground. "'At's what I wanna know. Eh, and check this out: Today I found a—"

Eyes on her, I stepped into thin air.

Oomph! I landed on hard ground.

"Let me guess," I said. "You found a hole?"

Ms. DeBree covered a smile with her paw.

I brushed myself off and stood up in the crater. "Just wanted a close-up look," I said.

Natalie smirked. "And who says you can't walk and detect at the same time?"

The hole opened into a tunnel. It headed far out under the playground.

"Holy Mole, Batman," said Natalie in an aw-shucks, Boy Wonder voice. "Someone's been burrowing."

"I can dig it," I said. "But who?"

"Ms. Burrower's a mole," said Natalie.

Maureen DeBree shook her head. "Nah, I checked. Her tunnels go between the teachers' lounge and her classroom, that's all."

"Hang on," I said. "We don't even know if this is connected to the classroom vandalism. One case at a time."

Ms. DeBree's tail bristled. *"Hmph!"* she snorted. "Who's asking you to solve a case? I'll figure this bugger out on my own. Just thought you wanted to see the vandalism."

She stomped off in a medium-sized huff, muttering to herself.

Way to go, Chet.

Natalie shook her head. "You are a smooth one with the ladies."

The bell rang. Lunch was over, class was calling.

"Let's pick it up at recess," I said, raising my arms. "C'mon, Natalie, give me a hand."

Natalie clapped slowly. That joke was older than my dad's GI Gecko doll, but she cackled over her own wit.

I scrambled out of the hole all by myself.

As I climbed, I thought, *You can't buy a partner like Natalie.* And what's worse, you can't even sell them.

11

Here a Wolf, Were a Wolf

Since I couldn't think of any way out of it, I headed back to my classroom for a double dose of science. With Science Fair happening tomorrow night, we were spending extra time working on our projects.

The excitement was so thick you could cut it with a blunt instrument. I half wished someone would use that blunt instrument on my head, to save me from working on our dumb project.

My group was buzzing. Shirley Chameleon and Tiffany the toad pushed two desks together and started laying out materials. Rynne Tintin hoisted a fresh sack of vegetables.

Only a miracle could save me from death by boredom.

It came.

A sixth-grade hall monitor slouched up to Mr. Ratnose's desk and handed him a note.

"Chet Gecko," said Mr. Ratnose, "report to the principal's office."

Sweeter words were never spoken. Better a quick death by bawling out than the slow torture of trying to get a charge from brain-dead vegetables.

Shirley rolled one eye at me. "What have you done now?"

"Don't ask," I said.

"'Don't ask,' you don't know, or 'Don't ask,' I don't want to know?"

I frowned. "Just *don't ask*."

Dames.

It was a piece of cake to walk up to Principal Zero's office. Knocking on his door was a banana split with fudge on top.

But walking inside and facing down that massive tomcat was a whole 'nother can of cherries.

"Come in," a voice rumbled.

Principal Zero's office smelled of broken dreams and old report cards, of kitty litter and fear. I opened the heavy oak door and stopped cold.

"You sent for me?" I asked.

A huge white cat sat behind a desk as heavy as a

cheater's conscience. He offered a smile as clear and innocent as a used car salesman's—only, Principal Zero's grin was crusted with flecks of old tuna fish.

"Sit down, Chester."

I hate it when they use my full name.

The guest chair before his broad black desk creaked as I sat. I didn't know what I'd done wrong, but I'd learned never to bring up my misdeeds before he did.

Principal Zero stared down at me. I stared back.

"You're probably wondering why you're here," he said. "It's . . ."

I broke. "I was nowhere near there at the time."

". . . a small matter we need your assistance with," he said. "Um, what did you say?"

"Oh, nothing."

I replayed his words. Wait a minute—Principal Zero asking for *my* help? That sounded screwier than a cage full of waltzing mice.

"Go on," I said.

Mr. Zero smoothed his whiskers. He waved a paw. "Perhaps Ms. LaRue should explain."

From a shadowy corner of the office strolled Heidi LaRue, a sixth-grade teacher all the kids called "Boom-Boom"—but never to her face, and always in whispers.

Ms. LaRue was a hefty hedgehog with a prickly

disposition and a glance sharp enough to cut you down to size and trim the hedges, both. Her classroom ran on iron discipline.

Of all the no-nonsense teachers at Emerson Hicky, she was the no-nonsense-iest—which made her next words even stranger.

"Earlier this morning," she said, "I saw a werewolf on campus."

I blinked. Either Popper's friend wasn't the only one seeing monsters, or the cafeteria was putting something funky into the applesauce.

"Where?" I asked.

"That's right, a *were*wolf," she said.

"No, *where* did you see it?"

"By the, uh, cafeteria, before school," said Ms. LaRue. Her lips shriveled like she'd kissed a moldy prune. "It was ugly and hairy—a great brute."

"Most of them are," I said.

Her mouth drew even tighter. Principal Zero coughed a warning.

"So what was it doing?" I asked.

Ms. LaRue glared. "It was wolfing about, of course!" She turned to the principal. "Honestly, Mr. Zero, I don't see what help this child can be. This is a matter for the authorities."

Principal Zero's tail twitched like a worm on a hot plate. Ms. LaRue's quills stood on end. He matched her glare for glare.

"This is *my* school, Ms. LaRue," he purred menacingly, "and *I* decide when to call the police."

This was kind of fun. Usually the teachers threatened *me*.

Finally, the hedgehog backed down. Her quills lay flat.

"Very well," she said. "But know this: Someone at school brought that creature here. Some so-called scientist is playing with forces they cannot control. And I won't have it."

Stiff and chilly as a grasshopper Popsicle, Heidi LaRue turned and stalked through the open door.

"And why do you think that?" I called after her.

The hedgehog turned up her nose. "Teacher's intuition." Then she spun and left us.

Mr. Zero leaned forward, his broad belly mashing the desk. "I don't have to tell you to keep this under your hat," he said. "Do I?"

I gave him my wide-eyed look. "Do you think there'll be room enough under it for everybody?"

The principal's whiskers bristled. "Gecko, I'm only calling you in on this because you're a low-down snoop. And you've done some successful snooping in the past."

"So what's my pay?"

"The satisfaction of a job well done," said Principal Zero.

"I can't get no . . . satisfaction," I said.

He stood. "Find out the lowdown on this werewolf and tell me—only me."

"And what if the story slips out?"

"No slips," he growled, "if you want to stay at this school."

That straight line was too easy. I let it slide and watched the big cat stew.

His eyes narrowed to slits, and his ears went back. "Mrs. Crow," rumbled Principal Zero to his secretary, "would you show Gecko the door?"

"I can find it myself," I said. "I'm a detective."

12

Jack and the Beans' Talk

Strolling back to class, I twirled my hall pass and chewed over what I'd heard. I knew why Principal Zero wanted to keep this werewolf thing quiet.

Full moon was tomorrow night—the night of Science Fair. If some supernatural critter terrorized the big event, the school supervisor would bust Mr. Zero from fat cat to alley cat quicker than you can say *kitty litter.*

My feet carried me toward Mr. Ratnose's room. But I stopped just down the corridor. I looked at the hall pass in my hand.

How often do you get a pass from a principal? A smile tugged at my lips. I'd be going back to class the long way.

By the time you reach second grade, you start to learn the ropes. If you need nursing, see the nurse. If you seek aggravation, bug a vice principal. If you want the lowdown, ask a librarian.

I eased open the library door. The air was chilly as a truant officer's smile. I caught a whiff of old books, fried brain cells, and high-test espresso.

Cool Beans was Emerson Hicky's head librarian and resident expert on the supernatural. An opossum the size of a refrigerator, he had a head for strange facts and a body for ripping phone books in half.

He was as hard to miss as a stegosaurus on a sesame-seed bun.

Cool Beans was shelving books. His sleepy eyes surveyed me from behind wraparound shades.

"What's the word, Winston?" he rumbled. "Did you fall by for a good book?"

"No, I need the hot scoop on a bad wolf."

"Lay it on me."

I pushed back my hat. "I've heard reports of a werewolf, or a were-hamster—something like that, on campus. Is it possible?"

Cool Beans lifted a lazy paw to scratch under his blue beret. "Wolves are scarce round here, but there's more wild things in this wigged-out world than you can even imagine, daddy-o. And that's the word from the bird."

"Huh?"

"It's possible."

Questions chased each other like kindergartners after an ice-cream truck. I picked one. (A question, not a kindergartner.)

"But a were-*hamster*?" I said. "I've only heard of were*wolves*."

Cool Beans pointed at a book on the cart. I passed it to him. As he slipped it into place, he said, "There's all kinds of were-critters—wolves, bears, frogs, even bunnies. Why not a hamster?"

"But *were*?"

"Anywhere, man."

I shook my head. "No, I mean, what makes an animal *were*?"

"Oh, a curse, sometimes, or a bite from another were-thing. It bugs 'em out, makes 'em wild."

At this, an inner door opened and a student entered. She shuffled along, head down, a hamster with glasses and curly brown—a *hamster*?!

I leaned toward Cool Beans and whispered, "Don't look now, but there's a hamster behind you."

He turned.

"I told you not to look," I said. "That could be the were-hamster."

The big possum chuckled. "What, Lauren? Man, are you blowin' on the wrong kazoo. Lauren Order is my assistant. She's a were-critter like I'm the ringmaster of a flea circus."

All the same, I kept an eye on her. Lauren nodded to the librarian and mumbled, "Omga gabacca brewers shastnow."

"Huh?" said Cool Beans and I together.

"Gonna go back to Ms. Burrower's class now," she repeated, slightly louder.

"All reet, sugar beet," said Cool Beans. "Catch you on the flip side."

She slipped out the door as softly as a ghost's whisper. I handed the possum another book. He cocked his massive head.

"A were-thing at school, huh?" he muttered. "What do you know?"

I cleared my throat. "So do these were-creatures stay that way all the time?"

"Naw, just for a few nights around the full moon," he said. Cool Beans patted the book. "Rest of the time, they're just regular goofs."

I leaned forward. "So if this were-creature is just a normal animal in the daytime, how am I supposed to find it?"

He grinned. "I dunno. You're the gumshoe, Jackson. I'm just a librarian."

"Thanks for reminding me," I said. "Sometimes I forget."

13

Lower the Boom-Boom

After the cool cave of the library, the sun's heat slapped my face like a spurned cheerleader. I squared my shoulders and plowed onward. It takes more than a sunny day to stop this private eye.

The halls were empty—just the way I like them. I decided to stretch my luck by making one more stop before returning to class.

Just down the hall from the library, the cafeteria squatted like a happy hippo, widemouthed and full of interesting smells. I smiled. Might as well grab a snack and check for evidence at the same time.

First I headed for the kitchen, where I knew the cafeteria ladies would give me a warm welcome.

But before I could step inside, I met a chilly attitude.

"You there, Gecko!"

It was Ms. LaRue, just leaving the cafeteria, as warm and cuddly as a king-sized cactus in high heels. She nibbled a grub-worm cookie and wore her usual frown.

"What are you doing here?" she asked.

"Well, I—"

"Get back to class at once. You can detect on your own time."

I knew that look in her eyes. I'd get as far arguing with Ms. LaRue as I would trying to tow the entire football team in a little red wagon.

"Then I guess this is where we say so long," I said.

She snarled in response. I didn't know a hedgehog could snarl.

"As they say in Rome, *Harry Verducci.*" I turned and ambled back to class, wondering idly why she didn't want me detecting just then. *Hmph.* There's just no pleasing some teachers.

Mr. Ratnose's classroom was as full of fun as a warm bucket of boogers. Most of the kids stood in tired clusters around their science projects—except for the oddballs like Igor Beaver, who were rootin'-tootin' and rarin' to go.

Shirley Chameleon looked up as I slid into my seat. "So what did Principal Zero want?"

In the next group over, Bosco made with the radar ears. "Just the usual," I said. "A mean tongue-lashing, followed by a serious tail chewing."

"*Eeew*," said Rynne Tintin. "Sounds painful."

"You don't know the half of it, sister."

Igor wrung his paws together. "People, please. Can we get back to work?"

I rolled my eyes and prepared to dive into Dullsville. But just then, another miracle occurred: recess.

A massive sigh of relief blew like Hurricane Jezebel through the room. I wove between the departing kids and headed for the candy machine. This having two cases at once was working out just fine. Now if I could only figure a way to get out of the rest of my classes. . . .

I fed my quarters into the slot, popped the button, and grabbed a Sowbug Twinkie. As I peeled back the wrapping, a familiar face poked through the passing crowd.

"Hey, Chet," said Natalie. "Do you know what the guests sang at the Eskimo's birthday party?"

"No, and I'm not sure I want to."

"*Freeze a jolly good fellow,*" she sang. "Get it?"

Mockingbird humor is an acquired taste. I hope I don't acquire it any day soon.

"Time for a powwow," I said.

"Lead the way, chief."

Munching on my treat, I steered us through a

pack of playful mice. We flopped down on the grass beside the sandbox. I savored each bite of the snack while Natalie filled me in on Bosco's latest activities: bullying, bribery, and shakedowns.

She said he'd even jammed up the drinking fountains with peanut butter. That reminded me of something, but I couldn't place it.

"So he—*mmm*—didn't do anything suspicious, eh?" I said.

"Just the usual. Now stop stuffing your face and explain this whole werewolf deal."

I stopped stuffing. I gave Natalie the lowdown from my meetings with Cool Beans and Principal Zero. Then my eyes wandered back to my half-eaten Twinkie.

Natalie sat up quickly. "When was this werewhatever first spotted?"

"Um, yesterday, I guess."

"And when did the vandalism start?"

"Yesterday."

"*Hmm . . .*" She leaned forward. "Chet, are you thinking what I'm thinking?"

"I doubt it. I was wondering how they get the sow bugs into the filling of the Twinkie."

Natalie frowned. "Chet!"

"Sorry," I said, gulping the last of my snack. "You were saying?"

My partner hopped up and began to pace. "Don't you see? This were-creature could be the one who's wrecking classrooms and—"

"And digging holes?" I asked. "Come on. What is this, *Revenge of the Were-Gopher?*"

"I don't know," said Natalie. "But there's one way to find out."

"There certainly is," I said. "What is it?"

Natalie's eyes glittered. "We stake out the school and catch it in the act."

I scratched my head. "And when we find out the truth—that the *gang* is actually doing the vandalism?"

"Then we hope they don't catch us first," she said. "Simple."

. . . As tap dancing through a minefield.

14

Oh, What a Dutiful Mornin'

Time spent on stakeout is as long and lonely as a python without a date. After school, Natalie and I discussed the best time for our surveillance. I voted for nighttime.

"There's only two problems with that," said Natalie.

"Oh yeah?" I said.

"Your mom and my mom."

"Oh yeah," I said. "So that leaves..."

A grin stretched across Natalie's beak. "Early morning. My favorite time of day."

Morning—*yuck*. What a rotten way to start the day. Still, if it would help us solve two cases at once, I'd march down Main Street with purple underwear on my head.

Or . . . maybe not.

Anyhow, much as I hated to admit it, Natalie was right. We agreed to meet before sunrise the next day.

"Cheer up, Chet," she said. "Early to bed and early to rise—"

"Makes a guy's eyeballs spin counterclockwise," I said. "Spare me the poetry. See you in the morning."

Next day, I told my mom I had to be at school early, to study. Strangely enough, she believed me. My skateboard waited in the garage. I dropped it in the driveway, hopped on, and rolled down the dark streets in a stupor, like a mummy on wheels.

If I never wake up that early again, it'll be too soon.

But early as it was, Natalie waited by the flagpole.

"Good morning, sunshine!" she chirped. "Ready to catch a monster?"

"Ready to catch some more z's," I muttered. "Where's that walkie-talkie?"

We each took one of the radios and headed for opposite ends of the school, to spread a wider dragnet.

Yellow security lights cast deep shadows. The sky was the color of burnt toast. An almost-full moon leered at me like a game-show host.

Minutes stretched like lazy cats. Nothing stirred. Even Maureen DeBree hadn't arrived yet.

I sat on my skateboard and tried to keep my eyes open. From far away came the siren song of my own sweet bed. *Sleeeep, beeeoootiful sleeeep,* it sang. I started to hum along, when a rude noise startled me awake.

Kkzzsch! "Come in, Chet. Over." It was Natalie's voice on the walkie-talkie.

I thumbed the talk button. "Yeah, what is it?" I yawned.

"Chet, you're supposed to say *over* when you're done talking. Over."

"*Over.* Over."

"Ha, ha," said Natalie. "All quiet here. Anything happening there? Over."

I scanned the empty school yard. "Nothing shaking but the leaves on the trees."

Natalie's voice came back, the only sound in the lonely predawn. "Let's check in later. Over and out."

"Roger, dodger," I said, just for yuks. I thought I heard Natalie snort, but it could have been static.

I set down the walkie-talkie and propped my elbows on my knees. Being a private eye isn't all glamour and gunshots, you know. Sometimes you've got to face down Mean Old Mr. Boredom on a stakeout.

If I kept sitting, sleep would claim me soon. I stood and stretched. My joints popped like an army of cheerleaders in a gum-chewing contest.

Couldn't hurt to take a spin past the library, I thought. Stepping onto my skateboard, I drifted down the hallways. I'd like to say my eyes were peeled and my senses were alert, but Mom always tells me not to lie. My brain felt like it had been wrapped in cotton and dipped in molasses.

Nothing happening by the library, either. I sat down again to keep watch. I watched my eyelids droop, lower... lower....

I was dreaming. I dreamed a huge shadow freed itself from the darkness of a nearby wall and flowed

across the grass. Closer and closer it came, easing toward me. I sat frozen.

The shadow loomed over me, its red eyes gleaming. It opened a wide, fanged mouth that smelled of... peanut butter?

"Yaaah!" I screamed, snapping out of my trance.

I found myself face-to-face with the were-creature of Emerson Hicky.

It was real.

15

Monster Mashed

"*Aieee!*" keened the startled monster. All I saw was fur and fangs.

It leaped backward like an Olympic gymnast in instant replay. By the time I staggered to my feet, the hairy creature was galloping for the administration building in a blur of speed. I pushed my skateboard in pursuit.

Then I thought, *What happens if I catch it?*

I needed backup. Rounding the corner, I pawed my pocket for the walkie-talkie. The monster had nearly made the shadows of the admin building.

Whizzing down the hall, I fumbled for the radio's talk switch. Where was—ah, found it!

"Natalie, come—"

Bwa-gonnng!

Unfortunately, I also found a pole.

The world spun like a whirling dervish playing Twister. I watched it spin. I wondered why the air felt so hard under my back. Oh yeah. It was the ground.

Head ringing, I picked myself up from the cement. Through the dizziness, a voice in my head repeated my name. Was I cracking up?

"Chet! Chet, what's happening?"

I grabbed my throbbing skull to silence the voice and found . . . I was wearing a walkie-talkie for a hat.

Natalie spoke again. "Chet? Come in, Chet!"

I clutched the radio to my face and thumbed the button. "You're supposed to say *over*," I groaned.

"THAT'S NOT FUNNY! OVER!" she yelled.

I held the walkie-talkie away from my ear. "Settle down," I said.

"I was worried about you, you nincompoop! Over!"

"I saw the monster. By the admin building."

"Why didn't you say so?"

By the time Natalie flapped up, I had gotten myself back together—or as together as I get, anyway. I scanned the shadows, but nothing moved.

Carefully, we circled the building. The creature's gunboat-sized pawprints led up to some bushes by the teachers' lounge. Then they stopped.

The monster was too big to hide behind a shrub. Had it leaped to the roof? I climbed the wall and poked my head over the top. Nothing.

Natalie took wing and scouted the area. Still nothing. For the next half hour, as teachers arrived and the sky grew pink, we searched the grounds.

Finally, we admitted it: The creature had given us the slip.

Discouraged, Natalie and I hunkered down on a wall at the edge of the playground. Students trickled onto campus.

The rascal moon slunk below the rim of the hill. I could have sworn the Man in the Moon was sticking out his tongue.

"Well," said Natalie, "what now, hotshot?"

I frowned. "I don't know what now. Cool Beans says that were-creatures only come out at night. So we can't track the monster till sundown."

She cocked her head. "True...but we don't know for sure that the monster's causing the vandalism...."

"So we go back to Plan B," I said, standing up. "We keep the squeeze on the Stinkers."

"And hold our noses," Natalie cackled.

I squared my shoulders and gave myself a pep talk. We were doing this for our school, we were doing this for my teacher—but most of all, we were doing this for the doughnuts. *Yum.*

We made for the portable buildings. All around us, the school was waking up in earnest. Passing sleepy students in the corridor, I figured we had just enough time to grill a gang member before class started.

The morning bell disagreed. *Rrrring!*

As I grumpily trudged to class, I thought, *There's*

a word for someone who lets bells boss him around. I slid into my seat and remembered what it was: a *dingbat.*

Morning recess was as welcome as the first sip of stinkberry milk shake after a brisk crawl across the desert. Kids poured out the door. I squeezed between them, eager to find Natalie.

Just as I was about to make tracks, someone tugged on my tail.

"Hey!" I said, trying to break free. "Easy; that thing comes off."

"Really? Let's see," a voice said.

I twisted around. Bosco Rebbizi had a fistful of tail. I jerked it from his paws.

"Sorry, only one per customer."

I eyeballed the ferret. Suspicion clung to him like stink on a skunk. (Of course, he *was* a Stinker.) Still, it couldn't hurt to ask about the latest vandalism.

"So," I said, "nice job with the holes in the playground."

He gave me a dead-eyed look. "What holes?" asked Bosco. "The only hole I know is the one in your head."

Everybody's a comedian.

"Where you been?" he demanded. "And what about your mean stunt?"

"Um, we want to make sure it's a really good—er,

bad one. In fact, I'm going to the library right now to research it. Bye."

Bosco grabbed my shoulder and spun me to face him. "Having second thoughts, Gecko?" he asked. "Trying to weasel out of it?"

I narrowed my eyes. "No, that's your department."

He stuck his face in mine. *Whew!* Bosco's breath smelled like something even a dingo wouldn't touch. "Meet us by the portables after lunch," he snarled. "Be there."

I unpeeled his fingers from my coat. "Only if you brush after eating," I said.

The ferret grunted and swaggered off. I watched him go, then shrugged. Time to follow our other lead and learn more about my supernatural encounter.

Natalie was lounging by the library doors. "Come on," I said. "Let's go in and tell Cool Beans about the were-critter."

"It wouldn't be much of a conversation," said Natalie.

"Why not?"

"He called in sick today," she said.

Dang. Sometimes a detective can't even detect. When that happens, I do what all great private eyes do.

I go play on the swings.

16

Auld Lang Gang

When gypsy-moth tacos perfume the air and horsefly brownies wait on a plate, how bad could life be? I won't say that food cures all ills, but it sure helps a detective get through the no-clues blues.

I savored lunch to the last nibble. Wiping my mouth, I pushed back the tray. "Bring on the bad guys; I'm ready to rumble."

Natalie cocked her head. "You look ready to urp," she said. "How could you have eaten that third brownie?"

"Alimentary, my dear Watson. Now, let's pay the gang a little visit."

Natalie and I strolled toward the portable buildings. (But how portable are they, really? Have you ever tried to lift one?) On the way, we debated what to tell Bosco and company.

"Why don't we say we're going to sell spittlebug cookies to raise money for the gang?" said Natalie.

"Hmm, I don't think that's what Erik had in mind."

We turned a corner and came upon Ms. LaRue and the janitor, Luke Busy, talking nose to nose. She started. He growled.

"What are you sniffin' around for, peeper?" said Luke Busy. The muscles in his shoulders humped, like camels doing the limbo under a blanket.

"I go to school here, remember?" I sneered.

Tough guys always set me off.

A leer played over his long snout. "Keep on wisecrackin', and you might get what's comin' to you," said the badger. Ms. LaRue's spikes rose, then flattened again.

"Oh yeah?" I said. "And you might hit a home run with a spaghetti noodle. But I doubt it."

Natalie pulled my arm and dragged me past them. "Come on, Chet."

Luke Busy snorted. "Some other time, Gecko—when I've got less on my mind."

"Could there be any less?" I said.

The big badger snarled. Ms. LaRue put a paw on his arm. "Down, Luke," she hissed. The hedgehog gave us a rusty smile. "He's, uh, cleaning up my classroom; it looks like it was vandalized by a wild animal."

More vandalism? I stared. This school was turning into a bigger disaster zone than my last report card.

"G'wan, beat it," said Luke.

He had a point. We beat it.

Natalie and I slipped behind the portables to meet the Dirty Rotten Stinkers. We slouched like punks and sneered like punks. We thought we were pretty tough.

We were sadly mistaken.

"Gecko and bird!" barked Erik. "C'mere!"

With attitude to spare, we strutted over to the giant tarantula.

"Time's up, punks," he rumbled. "What's yer dirty trick gonna be?"

Just then a familiar green face poked around the corner. "Chet?" It was Shirley Chameleon.

"Not now, Shirley," I said.

She batted her eyes. "I thought maybe we could study English together," she said, turning a lovely rose color. "That is, if you can spare some time from Mr. Ratnose's case."

Bosco's eyes narrowed. "Wait a minute, are you still doing that goody-good private eye stuff?"

"Uh, I—"

Shirley smiled. "He sure is. Chet's the best detective at Emerson Hicky."

I had to admit it, she was right. But her timing stunk.

Kurt the rat flashed a grin full of used grease and broken glass. "Awww, ain't that sweet? The teacher's pet."

He held Mr. Ratnose's pointer and tapped it meaningfully against his other paw. Bosco, Erik, and a couple of other mugs started drifting toward us. Storm clouds gathered in their faces.

I hooked a thumb at Shirley. "Don't listen to her," I said. "She's just a dame, see?"

Both Natalie and Shirley turned on me, outraged. "Hey!" they said together.

Suspicion sprouted like toadstools among the gamy gang.

"Ya tried to worm yer way in," Erik rumbled.

"You spied on us," said Bosco.

"You're no Stinkers, you stinkers!" said Kurt.

I looked at Natalie.

Uh-oh. The jig was up. Time for us to get jiggin'.

I turned a broad smile on Bosco and Erik. "Well, I've had a wonderful time," I said. "But this wasn't it."

"Aargh!" A snarl of frustration ripped from a

dozen throats. Couldn't ask for a better exit cue than that.

I snatched the pointer from Kurt's paws.

Natalie took to the sky; I took to my heels. Shirley stepped back. Dirty Rotten Stinkers swarmed after us like army ants after the Gingerbread Man.

They chased me down the hall, over the library, and out across the playground.

My breath grew short; I had more pants than a department store's menswear sale. The extra brownies sloshed in my gut, and my side burned with a dull fire.

"There he goes!" echoed behind me. I rounded a corner at top speed. I had just seconds to find a hiding place, but only one suggested itself: the Dumpster.

I climbed, held my nose, and dove.

Fshoomp!

The rotting garbage embraced me as tenderly as a mama skunk holds a rotten egg.

Ugh. The things I do for detection.

17

Ratty, Set, Go

After spending the rest of lunchtime buried under slimy leftovers, I needed a bath, a nap, and to have my head examined.

Instead, I shuffled back to class.

My aroma went before me. Thoughtful students cleared extra space around my desk. Even Shirley Chameleon kept her cooties to herself.

And Bosco? He sat in his chair, glaring. That ferret gave me an evil eye so mean, it made the Big Bad Wolf look like a pound puppy. But as long as we were in class, he couldn't lay a glove on me.

Probably.

"Bosco Rebbizi," said Mr. Ratnose. "Eyes front!"

Sometimes, it helps to have a strict teacher.

"Uh, Mr. Ratnose?" I asked.

"Yes, Chet Gecko?"

"I found your pointer in the trash."

He took it from me, holding the rod at arm's length. "Hmm. So I smell," he said.

The class broke into groups. We were supposed to put the finishing touches on our projects for that evening's Science Fair.

But all the time, my mind was burrowing through the litter of clues I'd uncovered.

Questions ping-ponged through my head. *How can I prove that Bosco trashed the classroom—or was it the were-thing? Will the were-whatsit rampage tonight? And how the heck do you spell* photosynthesis?

Some key was missing—a connection between all the weird events of the past few days. But it stayed even farther away than my stinked-out classmates.

At recess, I sat inside with an open book, pretending to study. Bosco and some Stinkers taunted me through the open door: "Chicken Gecko! *Bwak, bwak!*"

After Mr. Ratnose shooed them off, he shot me a strange look.

"What, you've never seen me study before?" I asked. "Maybe I'm turning over a new leaf."

"Mister, you'd have to turn over a whole tree."

My teacher wrinkled his nose. "By the way, how is my case coming?"

"I'm very close," I said, with a confidence I didn't feel.

Mr. Ratnose's ears twitched. "You'd better be. If you don't solve this case by tonight, our deal is off."

He shuffled back to his desk and began grading papers.

My box of doughnuts was going, going, gone. I wondered again: What was I missing? (Besides a mansion, my own TV show, and a lifetime supply of chocolate-covered dung beetles, I mean.)

When the last bell sounded, I glided out the door slicker than an eel on ice skates. Bending low, I crept through the crowd, leaving Bosco behind.

So far, so good.

I retrieved my skateboard and made it safely to a bush by the flagpole. Before long, my partner appeared.

"Natalie!" I hissed.

She joined me, and we ducked behind a hedge.

"There you—*whew!*" she said, fanning the air. "What, did they decide to make you a Dirty Rotten Stinker after all?"

"Ha, ha. I had to hide in the Dumpster to get away. How'd you escape?"

"Through the heating vents," she said. "So what now?"

"Time for drastic measures."

"We tell Principal Zero about the gang?" she asked.

"Not that drastic. No, we ambush a Dirty Rotten Stinker and squeeze some answers out of him."

Natalie grinned. "I'm your bird."

We peeked over the hedge at the kids leaving school. Soon, a likely target showed his snout: my old friend Kurt Replie. "Ready...," I whispered.

He drew even with us, then, "Go!" I hissed. Natalie and I jumped out and grabbed his elbows.

"We're doing a survey," I said. "How many Stinkers does it take to screw in a lightbulb?"

"Why don't ya—hey!" said Kurt the rat. "It's you!" He tried to wriggle free, but we held him in a vise grip.

Natalie and I steered our captive behind the bushes. Some curious passersby glanced our way, but knew better than to interfere. Nobody but a giraffe sticks his neck out at Emerson Hicky.

We braced the rat between us. His eyes jittered from Natalie to me. Like most bullies, he wasn't so tough without his gang.

"What do you want?" whined Kurt.

"Information," I said. "We wanna hear all about

how your buddy Bosco trashed Mr. Ratnose's classroom."

Bewilderment crossed the rat's face. You could tell it was a frequent visitor. "I dunno what you're talkin' about," he said.

"Don't playact with me," I sneered. "Give us the goods on Bosco, or else!"

"Or else what?" he asked.

I hate when they do that.

Just then, I glanced past his shoulder and saw an unfriendly face attached to an even less friendly body. It was Erik Nidd, patrolling and casting his many eyes around for . . . us!

"Aha!" shouted Erik.

"Uh-oh," said Natalie.

"Bye-bye," said I.

Just like that, Natalie and I skedaddled.

Erik chased us as far as the crossing guard. Then he shouted after us, "Ya can't hide forever. See ya at Science Fair!"

I wondered for a moment whether Principal Zero would be willing to transfer me to a nice safe school somewhere in Siberia—before six o'clock that evening.

Fat chance. Truth was, we were in deep, deep doo-doo.

18

What, Me Furry?

After a hot shower and a quick snack, I was nearly ready to face school again.

But first, dinner. Chez Gecko offered a tempting termite 'n' onion casserole, with candy-coated wasp eggs for dessert. *Mmm*. And the price was right: free.

"Chet," said my mom, "get right back here, and do these dishes."

Well, almost free.

As we drove to school, a fat gold sun hung just over the hills, like a sumo wrestler caught in a tree. Moonrise was near—and with it, the were-creature's return.

My parents and my sister, Pinky, dropped me at the auditorium. I waded through an anthill of activity to find Natalie before the program started. A couple of Dirty Rotten Stinkers crossed my path, but with their parents there, they could only scowl.

The cafeteria had been transformed into a giant laboratory from a mad scientist's dreams. Odd science projects from our class and others lined the walls. A huge, perpetual-motion wheel spun in the center of the room. Near it stood a scale model of a volcano and a water tank with a robot shark.

Drat! I *knew* our "Nature's Little Batteries" experiment was a dumb idea.

Natalie found me by the shark tank. "Listen," she said. "I've been reviewing our cases, and I think something big will happen tonight."

I blinked. "What do you mean?"

"Haven't you ever watched monster movies?" she asked.

"Yeah..."

Natalie leaned forward. "So, what did Godzilla do to Tokyo?"

"He trashed it," I said.

"And what did King Kong do to New York?"

"He wrecked it."

"And what does every werewolf do in every werewolf movie?"

I frowned. "They...scratch their fleas and howl?"

"No, you noodlehead," said Natalie. "They go on a rampage."

I put up a finger. "So you think maybe..."

"The monster's coming tonight," we said together.

Natalie nodded. "And I still think it did the vandalism. Remember, Ms. LaRue said her room had been torn apart by a wild animal. What could be wilder than a were-thing?"

"A bunch of Dirty Rotten Stinkers?" I scanned the cafeteria. "Anyhow, let's prepare for the worst. Where's Principal Zero?"

The huge cat stood chatting with a few teachers near the stage. As we approached, he was saying to Ms. Glick, ". . . and I'll bet she wins the Teacher of the Year Award for organizing this."

I think Ms. Burrower blushed. It's hard to tell with a mole. Boom-Boom LaRue looked like she had swallowed a pickled grub worm.

"Uh, Principal Zero," I said.

His tail twitched. "Not now, Gecko."

"It's about that . . . *thing* you asked me to do?"

Principal Zero frowned. He took my arm. "Excuse us, please, ladies," he purred. When we were alone in the corner, he growled, "What?"

"There *is* a were-something," said Natalie.

"A were-what?"

I shrugged. "We don't know, exactly. It was dark."

Principal Zero glanced around sharply. "Where is the creature now?"

"Uh, it gave us the slip."

His neck fur bristled. "You're the snoop," he said. "Go snoop around for it."

I jerked my head at the displays. "But . . . my science project?"

"Blast your science project," he snarled. "Find that were-thing before it finds us. Then call the janitors."

He didn't need to tell me twice; I'd rather snoop than science any day.

As I headed backstage to investigate, Natalie lagged behind. She eyed the exhibits longingly.

"What?" I asked.

"I'll . . . uh, watch the doors," she said.

I shook my head. My partner, the science nerd.

"Okay, but look sharp," I said. "We don't know which way this thing will jump."

I eased toward the curtains.

"Chet Gecko!" called Mr. Ratnose. "Go join your group."

"Can't," I said. "Principal's orders."

Mr. Ratnose's eyes narrowed. Much as I might have wanted to hear his discussion with Mr. Zero, it was time for action.

I slipped behind the curtains. The dust billowed. Hunting for a light switch, I shuffled along in the dimness.

From the corner of my eye, movement. I wasn't alone.

"Now we've got you!" crooned Bosco Rebbizi.

I backed away from him. A foot scraped behind me. I whirled.

A buff toad grinned at me—another gang member. I was trapped!

Zzwip!

I scaled the curtain in a flash, out of reach. Sometimes, it pays to be a gecko.

While Bosco and the toad fumbled for a ladder, I slithered through the gap in the curtains, slid to the floor, and ran into the crowded cafeteria.

Before they could track me, I shot out the door. Clouds filled the night sky. I looked both ways.

Now, where would a were-whatsit go to amuse itself? The swings? The library? The kennel?

I edged along the cafeteria wall, with one eye out for the monster and one eye out for gang members. This was one time it would've helped to have eyes like Shirley Chameleon's.

Turning the corner, I noticed an odd shape by the loading dock—some kind of tall box draped in cloth. As I moved closer, a twig cracked in the darkness.

There!—on the right—a dark figure loomed.

My quick gecko reflexes kicked in. I sprang to the wall.

A deep molasses voice drawled, "Like, take a chill pill, daddy-o."

"Cool Beans?"

"The real deal." The big possum ambled forward. "Now, what's the scam, Sam?"

I climbed down. "Looking for that werecreature," I said. "Hey, I thought you were sick?"

"Naw," said Cool Beans. "Just takin' a long nod back at my pad. Didn't want to miss the action. What's shakin'?"

"Nothing yet." I pointed at the tall box. "I was just about to check that out."

"Crazy, man. I'll cover you."

I walked up to the box and read a sign hanging on it: *Science Fair Property. Don't even think about opening this.*

I lifted an edge of the drapery. It revealed steel bars. I pushed the cloth higher and peered into the cage. It was darker than Dracula's belly button.

Hmm, a door.

Cool Beans spoke from behind me. "Should you be openin' that door, Sherlock?"

I opened it.

The moon appeared suddenly, and three things happened almost at once:

1) it shone on a furry shape inside the cage;

2) that furry shape blew up like a blimp in no time flat; and

3) it burst from the cage with an *"Eeeee!"* and bowled me over.

"I s'pose that answers my question," said Cool Beans.

19

Much Ado about Monsters

Tangled in the drapery, I sputtered, "After it!"
Cool Beans rushed to untangle me. An ice age
passed. Civilizations rose, flourished, and died a mis-
erable death. And still I was trapped.

"Hurry!" I said, struggling.

"Us possums only have two speeds," he said.
"This is the fast one, man."

Beyond the slow-moving librarian, the were-
thing disappeared around the building. Principal Zero
was going to kill me.

With Cool Beans's help, I unwrapped myself. He
was too slow; I'd have to chase down the monster
alone. "Call the janitors," I said. "I'll try to head
it off."

I charged after the were-creature, my coattails flying. Turning the corner, I skidded to a halt. The beast was standing under a tree. Monstrous, dark, and red eyed, the shaggy creature panted rapidly.

"Nice were-thingy," I said. The gentle touch works wonders.

It jumped like a frog on a whoopee cushion and tore away from me at top speed.

So much for the gentle touch. That thing was pretty skittish for a monster.

It dodged through a cafeteria door. I dashed into the room on its heels and smack into the middle of Pandemonium City.

The monster tore through the crowd like a hog through hog chow. Students and parents lunged out of the were-creature's way, trampling science projects and junior scientists alike.

"Stay calm!" shouted Principal Zero above the hubbub.

"My science project!" squealed Ms. Burrower.

Panting, I kept up the chase. The doorways were jammed with panicked kids; it couldn't escape. So the creature began tearing around the auditorium, running laps like a track star. No way could I tackle it. There had to be a better method for stopping it. . . .

Natalie was crouching by the perpetual-motion

wheel. I blinked. A brainstorm hit me. (It happens sometimes.)

I puffed up to her. "Natalie, when it comes around again, stand your ground."

"What?!" She looked at me like I'd flipped.

"Trust me," I said. "And make the loudest noise you can, on my signal."

She nodded shakily. I stepped aside and braced myself. Here came the marathon monster, barreling along.

It brushed past; I leaped behind it and spread my arms wide. "Now, Natalie!"

"*AAA-OOOOGAHH!*" she wailed, like a giant Klaxon.

Startled, the monster stopped dead. It whirled on me, and I flapped my arms, yelling, *"YAAAGH!"*

The were-creature turned again and half stumbled, half fell inside the spinning wheel. It scrambled to catch its balance. Then the monster dropped into a rhythm, running round and round inside the wheel, going nowhere fast.

The janitors arrived. Maureen DeBree and Luke Busy pushed through the crowd and stood waiting, armed with a net and rolls of duct tape. Gradually, the parents and kids overcame their fear and edged forward to watch. They murmured among themselves.

Ms. LaRue's bray cut through the noise like a hot sword through Jell-O. "I demand her resignation," she barked, stabbing a spiny finger at Ms. Burrower.

"Ms. Burrower's? Why?" asked Principal Zero.

"She created this, this *thing* as a science experiment, and endangered the whole school." Heidi LaRue bristled like an inside-out pincushion. "Someone could have been killed."

Mr. Zero turned to his Teacher of the Year. "Is this true?" he asked.

The mole blinked rapidly and lowered her head. "Aye," she said quietly. "It's my lunar transmogrification experiment."

The other teachers gasped and muttered among themselves.

"But I didn't intend to hurt anyone," said the mole. "I picked the quietest, mildest subject I could find: Lauren Order. And I kept her in my tunnels."

I flashed on the shy hamster I'd seen in the library, then looked at the huge hairy creature in the wheel. "*That's* a hamster?" I asked.

"A were-hamster, aye," said Ms. Burrower sadly. "The wee girl wouldn't hurt a fly; she only eats peanut butter and sunflower seeds."

Peanut butter and sunflower seeds? That rang a distant bell in my brain. But Ms. LaRue's buzz-saw voice drowned it out.

"Wouldn't hurt a fly, eh?" she said. "This unnatural creature has been vandalizing our school all week!" The hedgehog nodded, and Luke Busy stepped forward to grab Ms. Burrower's arm in one of his massive, clawed paws.

My brain churned. How could a *hamster* have done all that damage?

Mr. Ratnose looked from the were-hamster to me. "So *that's* the culprit," he said. "Fine detective you are, Chet Gecko."

I couldn't argue with that. Ah, well.

I had visions of doughnuts with little wings. They were flying away from me. I'd have to settle for my mom's peanut butter sandwiches. . . . Hey! *Peanut butter!*

"Wait just a minute," I said. "I know who the vandal is, and it's not the were-hamster!"

20

All Stinks Considered

A ring of astonished faces surrounded me. They all babbled at once like a passel of preschoolers at snack time.

"Impossible," said Ms. LaRue. "The creature's guilty; I know it."

"Explain yourself, Gecko," rasped Principal Zero.

I took a deep breath and hoped my mind could keep up with my mouth. "The hamster food, that's what tipped me off," I said.

"This is ridiculous," huffed the hedgehog. "Look at the creature's feet. There were huge, muddy footprints in the vandalized classrooms—exactly like tracks from those feet."

"Let him speak," said Mr. Zero.

I nodded and began to pace. "You see, when I checked out the wreckage in Mr. Ratnose's class, I found sunflower seeds, and on the wall, just a trace of peanut butter."

"That's right," said Maureen DeBree. "I saw the what-you-call, effervescence, when we was cleaning up."

"The *evidence,*" I said. "That's right—evidence that someone, or several someones, lured the were-hamster into the trashed classroom to frame her, and cover their own tracks."

I scanned the crowd. An angry face was blasting me with laser eyes: Bosco Rebbizi. If looks could fry, I'd be a crispy critter.

"The culprit or culprits," I said, "vandalized for their own twisted purposes." Erik Nidd crept up to the circle and stared daggers at me. The tension stretched like an overstrung rubber band.

"And the culprit is . . . ," I said, looking past Luke Busy to Bosco Rebbizi.

"It wasn't my idea!" Luke Busy exploded. "She made me do it, I swear!"

"Huh?"

The big badger pointed at Boom-Boom LaRue. "She wanted that Teacher of the Year Award, bad. She didn't want that mole lady to get it."

My head spun. "Right, so . . ."

"I did the damage," Luke said. "Those gashes in the wall, the tunnels on the playground—I did it all."

"You?" I said. "I mean, you! Because..."

The badger hung his massive, gray-striped head. "I'm just her smootchie-poo," he whispered. "I couldn't help myself."

"And that means...," said Natalie.

"Boom-Boom trashed the school to trash the mole lady's reputation." Luke Busy sighed.

Mr. Ratnose raised his eyebrows. "Darn, you're good," he muttered to me. I tipped my hat.

"Lies! All lies!" hissed Ms. LaRue, backing away. She turned to flee, then tripped over a net, expertly tossed by Maureen DeBree. "You'll hear from my lawyer."

"No," said Principal Zero, "we won't. But you might want to call him from jail."

A movement caught my eye. Luke Busy had taken advantage of the hullabaloo to sneak toward an open door.

"Stop him!" I shouted.

The badger made a break for it. Just then, Cool Beans materialized in the doorway. Luke Busy tripped over the possum's outthrust foot, and fell face first—*fwamp!*—knocking himself out cold.

Cool Beans sat on the soon-to-be ex-janitor.

"Thanks for the seat, Stan," he drawled. "I'm all flaked out from the chase."

While Maureen DeBree wrapped up the culprits in duct tape, Natalie and I had a heart-to-heart with my teacher.

"Pretty fancy detective work, I must admit," said Mr. Ratnose. Natalie nudged me. "So you knew all along it was the janitor, and you tricked him into confessing?" he asked.

I looked at Natalie, she looked at me. "Absolutely," we said together. Someone who won't tell a small fib for a box of jelly doughnuts doesn't want them bad enough.

As we wandered off into the crowd to find our families, Natalie and I were waylaid by two Dirty Rotten Stinkers: Erik Nidd and Bosco Rebbizi. I clenched my fists, my tail curled.

Bosco smiled. "So you wasn't a stool pigeon after all," he said. "I was wrong about you two."

Erik grinned, revealing more sparkly fangs than a vampire beauty pageant. "Were-hamster ruckus at Science Fair," he boomed. "Great stunt! Better than Bosco's. How'd ya like to be the newest Dirty Rotten Stinkers?"

I looked up at him and shook my head. "Not for all the cookies in Kowloon," I said. As we slipped past them, Erik turned in shock to Bosco. "I was gonna show 'em the secret claw-shake, an' every-thing..."

As the old saying goes, I wouldn't want to belong to any club that would take someone like me as a member. Besides—and I think Natalie would agree with me on this—better a snooper than a Stinker, any day.

Look for more mysteries from
the Tattered Casebook of Chet Gecko

Case #1 *The Chameleon Wore Chartreuse*

Some cases start rough, some cases start easy. This one started with a dame. (That's what we private eyes call a girl.) She was cute and green and scaly. She looked like trouble and smelled like . . . grasshoppers.

Shirley Chameleon came to me when her little brother, Billy, turned up missing. (I suspect she also came to spread cooties, but that's another story.) She turned on the tears. She promised me some stinkbug pie. I said I'd find the brat.

But when his trail led to a certain stinky-breathed, bad-tempered, jumbo-sized Gila monster, I thought I'd bitten off more than I could chew. Worse, I had to chew fast: If I didn't find Billy in time, it would be bye-bye, stinkbug pie.

Case #2 *The Mystery of Mr. Nice*

How would you know if some criminal mastermind tried to impersonate your principal? My first clue: He was nice to me.

This fiend tried everything—flattery, friendship, food—but he still couldn't keep me off the case. Natalie and I followed a trail of clues as thin as the cheese on a cafeteria hamburger. And we found a ring of corruption that went from the janitor right up to Mr. Big.

In the nick of time, we rescued Principal Zero and busted up the PTA meeting, putting a stop to the evil genius. And what thanks did we get? Just the usual. A cold handshake and a warm soda.

But that's all in a day's work for a private eye.

Case #3 *Farewell, My Lunchbag*

If danger is my business, then dinner is my passion. I'll take any case if the pay is right. And what pay could be better than Mothloaf Surprise?

At least that's what I thought. But in this particular case, I bit off more than I could chew.

Cafeteria lady Mrs. Bagoong hired me to track down whoever was stealing her food supplies. The long, slimy trail led too close to my own backyard for comfort.

And much, much too close to the very scary Jimmy "King" Cobra. Without the help of Natalie Attired and our school janitor, Maureen DeBree, I would've been gecko sushi.

Case #4 *The Big Nap*

My grades were lower than a salamander's slippers, and my bank account was trying to crawl under a duck's belly. So why did I take a case that didn't pay anything?

Put it this way: Would you stand by and watch some evil power turn your classmates into hypnotized zombies? (If that wasn't just what normally happened to them in math class, I mean.)

My investigations revealed a plot meaner than a roomful of rhinos with diaper rash.

Someone at Emerson Hicky was using a sinister video game to put more and more students into la-la-land. And it was up to me to stop it, pronto—before that someone caught up with me, and I found myself taking the Big Nap.

Case #5 *The Hamster of the Baskervilles*

Elementary school is a wild place. But this was ridiculous.

Someone—or something—was tearing up Emerson Hicky. Classrooms were trashed. Walls were gnawed. Mysterious tunnels riddled the playground like worm chunks in a pan of earthworm lasagna.

But nobody could spot the culprit, let alone catch him.

I don't believe in the supernatural. My idea of voodoo is my mom's cockroach-ripple ice cream.

Then, a teacher reported seeing a monster on full-moon night, and I got the call.

At the end of a twisted trail of clues, I had to answer the burning question: Was it a vicious, supernatural were-hamster on the loose, or just another Science Fair project gone wrong?

Case #6 *This Gum for Hire*

Never thought I'd see the day when one of my worst enemies would hire me for a case. Herman the Gila Monster was a sixth-grade hoodlum with a first-rate left hook. He told me someone was disappearing the football team, and he had to put a stop to it. Big whoop.

He told me he was being blamed for the kidnappings, and he had to clear his name. Boo hoo.

Then he said that I could either take the case and earn a nice reward, or have my face rearranged like a bargain-basement Picasso painted by a spastic chimp.

I took the case.

But before I could find the kidnapper, I had to go undercover. And that meant facing something that scared me worse than a chorus line of criminals in steel-toed boots: P.E. class.

Case #7 *The Malted Falcon*

It was tall, dark, and chocolatey—the stuff dreams are made of. It was a treat so titanic that nobody had been able to finish one single-handedly (or even single-mouthedly). It was the Malted Falcon.

How far would you go for the ultimate dessert? Somebody went too far, and that's where I came in.

The local sweets shop held a contest. The prize: a year's supply of free Malted Falcons. Some lucky kid scored the winning ticket. She brought it to school for show-and-tell.

But after she showed it, somebody swiped it. And no one would tell where it went.

Following a strong hunch and an even stronger sweet tooth, I tracked the ticket through a web of lies more tangled than a rattlesnake doing the rumba. But the time to claim the prize was fast approaching. Would the villain get the sweet treat—or his just desserts?

Case #8 *Trouble Is My Beeswax*

Okay, I confess. When test time rolls around, I'm as tempted as the next lizard to let my eyeballs do the walking . . . to my neighbor's paper.

But Mrs. Gecko didn't raise no cheaters. (Some language manglers, perhaps.) So when a routine investigation uncovered a test-cheating ring at Emerson Hicky, I gave myself a new case: Put the cheaters out of business.

Easier said than done. Those double-dealers were slicker than a frog's fanny and twice as slimy.

Oh, and there was one other small problem: The finger of suspicion pointed to two dames. The ringleader was either the glamorous Lacey Vail, or my own classmate Shirley Chameleon.

Sheesh. The only thing I hate worse than an empty Pillbug Crunch wrapper is a case full of dizzy dames.

Case #9 *Give My Regrets to Broadway*

Some things you can't escape, however hard you try—like dentist appointments, visits with strange-smelling relatives, and being in the fourth-grade play. I had always left the acting to my smart-aleck pal, Natalie, but then one day it was my turn in the spotlight.

Stage fright? Me? You're talking about a gecko who has laughed at danger, chuckled at catastrophe, and sneezed at sinister plots.

I was terrified.

Not because of the acting, mind you. The script called for me to share a major lip-lock with Shirley Chameleon—Cootie Queen of the Universe!

And while I was trying to avoid that trap, a simple missing persons case took a turn for the worse—right into the middle of my play. Would opening night spell curtains for my client? And, more important, would someone invent a cure for cooties? But no matter—whatever happens, the sleuth must go on.

Case #10 *Murder, My Tweet*

Some things at school you can count on. Pop quizzes always pop up just after you've spent your study time studying comics. Chef's Surprise is always a surprise, but never a good one. And no matter how much you learn today, they always make you come back tomorrow.

But sometimes, Emerson Hicky amazes you. And just like finding a killer bee in a box of Earwig Puffs, you're left shocked, stung, and discombobulated.

Foul play struck at my school; that's nothing new. But then the finger of suspicion pointed straight at my favorite fowl: Natalie Attired. Framed as a blackmailer, my partner was booted out of Emerson Hicky quicker than a hoptoad on a hot plate.

I tackled the case for free. Mess with my partner, mess with me.

Then things took a turn for the worse. Just when I thought I might clear her name, Natalie disappeared. And worse still, she left behind one clue: a reddish smear that looked kinda like the jelly from a beetle-jelly sandwich but raised an ugly question: Was it murder, or something serious?

Case #11 *The Possum Always Rings Twice*

In my time, I've tackled cases stickier than a spider's handshake and harder than three-year-old boll weevil taffy. But nothing compares to the job that landed me knee-deep in school politics.

What seemed like a straightforward case of extortion during Emerson Hicky's student-council election ended up taking more twists and turns than an anaconda's lunch. It became a battle royal for control of the school. (Not that I necessarily believe school is worth fighting for, but a gecko's gotta do something with his days.)

In the end, my politicking landed me in one of the tightest spots I've ever encountered. Was I savvy enough to escape with my skin? Let me put it this way: Just like a politician, this is one private eye who always shoots from the lip.

Case #12 *Key Lardo*

Working this case, I nearly lost my detective mojo—and to a guy so dim, he'd probably play goalie for the darts team. True, he was only a cog in a larger conspiracy. But this big buttinsky made my life more uncomfortable than a porcupine's underpants.

Was he a cop? A truant officer? A gorilla with a grudge? Even worse: A rival detective. His name was Bland. James Bland. And he was cracking cases faster than a . . . well, much faster than I was.

My reputation took a nosedive. And I nearly followed it—straight into the slammer. Fighting back with all my moxie, I bent the rules, blundered into blind alleys, and stepped on more than a few toes.

Was I right? Was I wrong? I'll tell you this: I made my share of mistakes. But I believe that if you can't laugh at yourself . . . make fun of someone else.